A GREEDY VICTORY OVER GOD

CHANDRAKAMAL AINNERI

Made with ♥ on the Notion Press Platform
www.notionpress.com

Contents

Foreword

Dear Reader,

A genuine thankyou from the bottom of my heart because you have purchased my first ever book.I have written this book with so much passion and intention to make someone think or at least to plant a thought in my audience's mind.

As you turn each page,you will discover both heartwarming moments and heart-wrenching twists. End of the day both should be part of our life's which makes "Life is beautiful", because You will appreciate the arrival of light when you are in the dark. I hope this book will keep you engaged. Please forgive me if there are any mistakesHave a great day champ :)

Please provide your valuable feedback at chandrakamal303@gmail.com

Source Of Inspiration

Just because we have more cognitive ability does not imply that we are a superior species. Natural resource extraction is occurring at a rapid pace. The statement "Earth is the planet of life" is gradually losing its meaning as humans, also known as devils, live here. In the sake of being the most intelligent species, we have gone beyond all limits. We are harming the ecosystem and causing new problems. The greed of humans has spread like wildfire, devouring everything in its path. Don't underestimate how horrible it is, when you realise you've turned into ash.

CHAPTER I

The Roar of Rebellion

As the evening sun went down behind the hills, sending out long streaks of light, As the lovely evening arrived, it was time to return to the nest for rest, the sounds of a waterfall and the melodies of birds welcomed the darkness of dusk.

a monkey perched on the edge of a cliff watched in terror as humans at the forest's edge were cutting down trees. Seized by fear, it immediately started to run, shouting along the way, "They have arrived, everyone follow me, quickly!" without revealing where it was heading, leading everyone in a hurried escape.

Birds, snakes, sparrows, deer, insects, and all the creatures of the forest gathered at the cave where the lion, though a king, had convened a meeting.

Despite being a king, the lion emerged from the cave, bluffing courage while hiding its fear, and looked seriously at everyone. However, the pain in the lion's eyes, stemming from its inability to protect the forest from humans, was evident to all the other animals.

Gathering some courage, the monkey said, "King, the rumours are true. Humans are planning to encroach our forest and build structures here. It's better for us to move to another area, otherwise they will ruthlessly kill us or capture us all."

Hearing this, all the animals became very frightened, lamenting their helplessness, "We have lived in this forest through hardships and happiness, do we now have to leave it because of humans?"

Realising what he feared most was becoming true, he pondered over the idea of leaving the forest as the monkey suggested. All the animals waited anxiously to see what decision the lion would make.

Lion looked at the elephants to know what they were thinking. Elephants tearfully said, "This land is where we were born, and if necessary, we will die here, but it's hard to leave our home."

"Yes, even if they capture us, they will imprison and torture us. It's better to fight for our forest and die than to live in bondage," said the buffaloes.

"This is our home, we must protect it," cried the birds and snakes, uniting in a chorus of revolutionary shouts.

Suddenly, the area was engulfed in the sound of revolution, resonating throughout.

Seeing the love the animals harboured for the forest, the lion was filled with joy...

As everyone continued their revolutionary cries, a loud roar was heard, silencing everyone. "We cannot fight the humans, they have machines. I have fought them before they are very powerful, and even your king knows this," declared the tiger as it entered the assembly.

The lion looked into the tiger's eyes and acknowledged the truth. "What should we do now?" asked the fox.

"We need to strike them cleverly. If we win the battle today and chase them away, more will come tomorrow to attack us. We must find a way to ensure they never invade our forest again," the tiger proposed.

"I know a solution," said the snake, to which all the animals eagerly asked, "What is it? What is that solution?"

"I live in the burrows of their village, and I've observed them many times. They have more faith in God than in themselves. We must use this belief to strike back," the snake explained. Indeed, "we also noticed that they believe God will provide for them effortlessly" stated by Monkeys.

Immediately, the lion had an idea, which he promptly shared in detail with all the animals. They listened attentively. Some were afraid, but all were united by the intention to save the forest.

"The plan must be implemented tomorrow," the lion declared his command.

CHAPTER II

Fooling the Mighties

Golden light spilled across the land, as the sun began its ascent., "Strange whispers carried on the wind, hinting at a new chapter in the forest going to begin...

Mallayya, like any other day, came into the deep forest to collect firewood and started his work. Everything seemed usual as he sang joyfully while working, but he was unaware that he was part of a larger plan.

As per the Plan, all the animals were waiting in their respective places, and upon receiving a signal from the lion, the strategy was executed.

The bear attempted to attack Mallayya, who ran in fear. The strategy involved leading Mallayya towards the edge of the forest, near a tree close to the village, without him escaping deeper into the forest. As the bear chased him, the snakes and foxes redirected Mallayya towards the intended edge of the forest.

As Mallayya was fleeing in fear, he saw the familiar outlines of a few houses from his village. Realising he was nearing safety, he thought he could easily escape the danger and return to his village. Once inside, he hoped to gather the villagers and deal with the bear threatening him. However, a large tiger suddenly leapt out, blocking Mallaiah's path. According to the animals' plan, they herded Mallayya towards a tree, leaving him surrounded with no way to escape.

Trembling with fear, Mallayya backed up only to realise he was trapped against a tree, feeling as though his end on this earth was near to him. Just then, the bear signalled to the monkeys above, who began pounding the tree trunk with a large branch. With a loud thud, a bark of the tree fell, and when Mallayya opened his eyes, he saw a figure of the Goddess on the tree, astonishing him. As he turned his head to look at the bear again, it bowed down as if paying homage to the Goddess and then fled the scene.

All the animals there, including the tiger, pretended to bow down to the goddess just like the bear did, and then fled from the spot. Seeing this, Mallya rejoiced, thinking he had escaped death.

Mallayya, overwhelmed with tears, thanked the goddess who saved his life, exclaiming, "The goddess saved me! The goddess saved me!" as he ran towards the village. Everyone in the village talked about Mallayya, and the matter reached the village council officials. They called Mallayya to tell them what happened. Mallayya recounted everything in detail, stating, "The goddess was in the tree, she saved me." The entire village debated whether Mallayya's story was true or false. Finally, the whole village headed towards the tree.

Informed by the birds that people were approaching the tree, the animals quickly prepared for their next move. As the people reached the tree, they were stunned to see an image resembling a goddess formed on its trunk. This extraordinary sight ignited belief among many of the villagers. Yet, the village officials, sceptical of the miraculous appearance, scrutinised the image closely. suggesting that someone must have crafted it with leaves to either create a hoax. Or Mallayya himself crafted this with twigs to gain recognition as a great devotee or to stir intrigue and admiration among the villagers. He proposed discussing the matter thoroughly at the village council. He suggested that this matter should be brought before the village council for a thorough investigation.

Mallayya countered, "No, it's genuinely the goddess who has manifested herself here to bless our village," amidst the chaos. Following the official's suggestion, the crowd decided to resolve the issue in the council and started heading back to the village.

Meanwhile, observing the unfolding events from a distance, the lion and the monkeys signalled to each other. Promptly responding, the monkeys replicated their earlier action by striking a nearby branch, causing it to fall. As the branch hit the tree, the bark that had concealed the engraving of the goddess on the tree trunk peeled away. The villagers, caught by surprise, were filled with awe. Their initial scepticism

melted away as they see the goddess shape on twenty trees at a time. They can't believe what they actually saw. They have been hit by a divine storm.This unexpected reveal stunned the villagers, turning their doubt into belief as they cried out, "Forgive us, Mother!" They were so moved by this experience.Convinced of the goddess's miraculous intervention, they started praying right there.

Convinced of the spiritual importance of this site, the village officials decided to build a temple there. They quickly began setting things up for the construction, declaring the place sacred. Mallayya was very emotional, believing the goddess had shown herself to him first, confirming his spiritual calling. The women of the village, inspired by what had happened, wore yellow traditional attires and took part in the religious activities with great devotion, feeling uplifted by the promise of divine protection and blessings.

As the villagers were deeply engaged in worship, they heard some other people nearby giving orders, "Clear everyone out quickly, this work needs to be done in two days," as they arrived with machines to cut down the forest.they were construction engineers.

"Why are you here?" asked the village officials.

"Don't you know? We already told you that we are going to cut down the trees in this forest to build buildings. You even asked us to give your villagers some work, so why are you asking now?" stated engineers

"I did say that, but now we can't agree to let you destroy this forest," the village guy responded, and a sense of joy began in the hearts of the animals listening secretly. Their eyes sparkled with the hope of victory.

"Why won't you agree?" the engineer asked.

"Look over there at the tree, the goddess has appeared here to protect our village, the divine power is hidden in this forest," they showed him.

They explained to the officials that the goddess had manifested to protect their village, urging them to stop their work and leave.

The engineers responded defiantly, "No, we will complete our work, what will you do about it?"

Hearing this, the villagers' anger boiled over. They started protesting with shouts, threw stones, and drove the officials away. Even when the police arrived, they fought to ensure that not a blade of grass in the forest was harmed by the officials, and the confrontation eventually reached the courts. The court considered the village's customs and the sanctity of the forest, ruling that the forest should not be touched. The engineers had to stop their work and leave.

The village burst into celebrations, but the animals in the forest celebrated even more. They had cleverly used leafy twigs to create an image of the goddess on the tree trunk, convincing everyone that the divine had intervened to save Mallayya, thus protecting their habitat, and animals thanked the lion who had orchestrated the plan. They were overjoyed that their problem was resolved and they could live happily in the forest.

"Start the festival for the goddess," the village officials announced. The villagers began the festival in grandeur and splendour.

CHAPTER III

God's Own Twist

As the people joyfully spent their days, they also visited the trees daily to worship the goddess depicted there.

Every two nights, the monkeys would freshen up the goddess's image on the tree using leafy twigs, ensuring it always looked vivid and worshipful.

The villagers were completely immersed in devotion, turning the area into a spiritual sanctuary filled with religious activities.

As time passed smoothly, both the people, with their prayers, and the animals, who had saved the forest, continued their lives. Just as it is true that there is light, it is equally true that darkness follows.

One day, during a festival for the goddess, while everyone was busy with the celebrations, something that looked like a muddy ball-like structure appeared at the base of the tree. When the priest inspected it, he discovered it was gold, almond sized, round close to a spherical shape . Everyone was amazed.

The villagers believed that the goddess had rewarded their festival with this gold gift. In reality, it was a ring belonging to Mallayya, which had slipped from his hand and fallen to the ground when he was being chased by the animals long ago. The ring had been crushed by the branches thrown by the animals and gradually buried in the soil. However, Mallayya was not around to explain this, as he had left on a pilgrimage to proclaim that the goddess had appeared to him personally. He left his village as he is on a journey to different parts of the country to announce himself that he is a messenger of god. The villagers continued to believe that the goddess had blessed them with the gold for protecting the forest and fervently conducting rituals and festivals in her honour.

As greed took root in their minds, the villagers made it a habit to hold a festival once a week, and they began to dig around the base of the tree regularly. With each weekly festival, the more they dug, the more the ground around the tree gradually began to sink.

Their obsession reached a point where they thought the goddess was not pleased with their regular festivals because no gold was found, leading them to believe that they needed to perform more extreme acts. They instituted a rule that every week, a woman from a household must walk over a fire pit, perform rituals, and together with her husband, who would fast for a week, they must sacrifice a goat. All these activities were closely observed by the animals from the forest. Monkeys and birds always relayed every detail to the lion. The animals laughed at the foolishness of the humans, but the lion began to feel a sense of dread that something terribly wrong was happening and warned everyone to be cautious.

Foolishness spread among the people like wildfire. Despite walking over fire pits and sacrificing numerous goats, no gold was found. They continued to dig at the base of the tree until it slowly began to collapse.

At the village council meeting, everyone gathered again.

Birds and monkeys perched quietly on nearby trees to listen in.

As the meeting started, discussions arose about why the goddess hadn't shown them mercy by giving them gold as before. One person expressed doubts about their religious offerings not being enough. Another suggested that perhaps providing human sacrifices would impress the goddess and bring gold. Some wondered if the delay in constructing the temple had angered her, leading to their current misfortunes. Amid these speculations, a woman suggested, "We've only ever dug under one tree. But there were around 30 tree's with goddess images, we didn't think of this, what if the gold is near the remaining trees?

Agreeing that they had overlooked other possibilities,and felt that finally an old woman thought can help us. Motivated by their disgusting hope the villagers decided to dig each and every tree with goddess images and search for gold, and the entire village headed to the forest with tools, ready to dig around more trees.

The animals, having learned of this through the birds, rushed to the trees in panic.

The excavation began, and as each person started digging around a different tree,

Seeing this, the lion became furious, its rage boiling over. Unable to tolerate the deception and fearing that the humans were destroying its forest, he ran out of ideas and quickly ordered the animals to attack the people.

Foxes and leopards positioned themselves defensively in front of the trees, guarding them. The people initially panicked, then grew suspicious, wondering how all these animals had gathered exactly here and why they were so fiercely protecting the trees. They strongly believed that the gold would definitely be here, and these animals were guardians appointed by the goddess to protect both her and the gold. They recalled how a bear had previously chased Mallayya until the bark of the tree split to reveal the goddess, after which the bear ran away. Post that the gold was found.

In the meantime, some leopards attacked the humans, and elephants along with other animals also joined in the assault. Unable to fend off these attacks, the people fled from the area.

CHAPTER IV

The last sunrise

The day the animals had always feared eventually arrived. All the animals gathered around the trees. The animals, who had believed that convincing the people of the goddess's presence in the forest would lead them to protect it with their devotion, found themselves unable to believe what they were now seeing.

Blinded by selfishness, greed, and foolishness, the villagers forgot the miraculous appearance of the goddess on the trees and performed a regrettable act. The machines were brought by the villagers from the same persons against whom they had protested in order to save the forest. Yes, they brought men and machinery to stop the animals from engaging in their despicable behaviour as the animals were refusing to let them dig close to the trees.

Witnessing this, the animals were heartbroken. Their faith in God seemed defeated by the humans' selfishness, leaving them feeling as if even divine power had lost to human greed.

The people started digging around each tree with machines. Those who had worshipped and pledged their devotion to the goddess during the festival were now uprooting the very trees that bore her images, all for a small piece of gold. Seeing their forest being destroyed right before their eyes, the animals were deeply distressed. They uprooted all the trees with images of the goddess, and finding nothing, continued their desperate search under other trees.

Unable to bear the devastation, the elephants attacked the people, but it was in vain. Some of the elephants were tied up with machines, while others were killed.

As humans cleared the entire end of the forest, digging up and ruthlessly killing any animal that got in their way, a final meeting took place among the surviving animals, led by the lion in the middle of the forest.

"I have failed, I couldn't protect you as the king of this forest. Forgive me," said the lion, bowing its head to the ground.

"I had warned before that we cannot fight against humans, but you didn't listen. Look now, many birds have lost their homes, elephants and leopards have died. What future do these animals have? All this is your fault," the lion accused.

"I admit, the fault is mine," the lion accepted the blame.

Then, as a king making its final command, the lion said, "Leave this forest immediately and move to the neighbouring forest." Unable to defy their king, all the animals started their journey to another forest, but the lion stayed.

"Enough grieving, now move," said the tiger.

"No, I am the king of this forest, and if I die, I will die here in this forest, in the fight to protect it. I cannot leave it. Because of my decision alone, so many animals have died. I will offer tributes with the blood of humans for the death of the animals I will fight until my last breath. As a king, this is my duty," said the lion. Seeing the passion in the king's eyes, the tiger was stunned.

"Has your mind dulled? They easily killed the elephants they will kill you too. All the other animals are moving to a new place; if you don't join them, they won't leave either. They will fight for you, do you want to be the reason for their deaths too? They are leaving to survive, and don't change their minds. There, they are calling for you, come," the tiger pleaded.

"You go and tell them that I will be spending some time in my cave and will be back soon," instructed the lion to the tiger, asking her to take everyone away from there.

With sorrow in his eyes, the tiger went to the other animals and when they asked where the king was, she explained, "The king wants to spend some time alone in his cave and has asked us to leave." Believing this, the animals left the forest and moved completely to another area.

Now, in that forest, there were only uprooted trees, large dug pits, the noise of machines, and people with corrupt minds, along with the lone lion.

People completely destroyed the forest, making their way to its central part. Over the months, performing rituals and sacrifices to resolve their hardships, lion watching humans continue to destroy his kingdom right before his eyes, they used machines to violently uproot trees all at once, digging the place like dogs scavenging for food, madly searching for gold as if it were guaranteed to be found there.

Seeing all this, the lion jumped on the people ferociously, wiping them out with his claws, witnessing the blood of everyone who came in his way. Everyone was terrified of the lion's ferocity for a moment. But unfortunately, the people quickly reacted and shot the lion with guns. The lion fell to the ground, riddled with bullet wounds.

They tied it to a large rock and also destroyed the rest of the forest. However, they could not find any traces of gold, even after thoroughly searching the entire forest. Now, the area is filled with piles of soil, holes everywhere, and uprooted trees. Some people felt sad that no gold was found, while others were angry. At that moment, everyone set fire to all the uprooted trees, even those where they had previously worshipped the goddess and had been protected from authorities. Seeing the same forest they had worshipped and protected now being destroyed by their own hands, the lion was devastated.

The pain from the betrayal hurt more than its physical injuries. The greed-induced fires consumed even the lion, the king of the forest. The lush forest, once vibrant with green trees now teeming with wildlife, was now a charred wasteland. This proved again that those with good intentions are often defeated. As evening fell, the forest was cloaked in complete darkness.

Months later, a group of twenty-story buildings named 'Nature's ornament" were constructed on the site, turning it into a blemish among the remnants of the forests.During the inaugural evening festivities atop the building's terrace,Builder with a handful of drink and mind full of mud asked an officer "Hey ,Imagine if we cleared the surrounding forest and constructed larger buildings for VIP clients. we could make a lot of money...."

www.ingramcontent.com/pod-product-compliance
Lightning Source LLC
Chambersburg PA
CBHW031256130726
47988CB00008B/3385